The Return of the Third-Grade Ghosthunters

by Grace Maccarone
illustrated by Kelly Oechsli
Cover art by Carol Newsom

A
LITTLE APPLE
PAPERBACK

SCHOLASTIC INC.
New York   Toronto   London   Auckland   Sydney

Here is another book
about the third-grade ghosthunters
that you will enjoy:

The Haunting of Grade Three
by Grace Maccarone

ISBN 0-590-41944-7

Copyright © 1989 by Grace Maccarone.
All rights reserved. Published by Scholastic Inc.
APPLE PAPERBACKS is a registered trademark of Scholastic Inc.

12 11 10 9 8 7 6 5 4 3 2 1   9/8 0 1 2 3 4/9

Printed in the U.S.A.   11

First Scholastic printing, September 1989

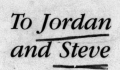

*To Jordan
and Steve*

Chapter One

GHOSTS, THOUGHT ADAM. They're everywhere. They're dancing behind your back, giggling behind doors, telling jokes under tables, even playing with the toys underneath the bed. Then, as soon as you turn to have a look, they're gone. They're quick — but not quick enough for Adam Johnson, third-grade ghost-hunter. Adam took aim with his ghostblaster.

"You got me!" It was Adam's brother, Tim.

"That shows how much you don't know," Adam said. "These ghostblasting rays are harmless to all living things. But, ghosts, watch out!"

Adam took aim again. "Got one!"

"Lights out!" Adam's mother called from the bottom of the staircase. "You have a big day ahead of you!"

Tomorrow would be no ordinary school day. Two of the third-grade classes were going on a trip to a real farm. They would sleep over for two whole nights.

Adam packed his ghosthunting things just in case he needed them:

A pad and a pencil to take notes;
A tape measure to find out if anything had been moved;
A camera and flash to take pictures;
A tape recorder to record strange noises;
A bag of flour to find human footsteps and fingerprints.

Adam was ready for adventure.

7

Chapter Two

ADAM LOVED scary things. He could think about ghosts and monsters during all his waking hours. But Adam liked to keep them out of his dreams.

Adam checked his room every night. He looked for ghosts, monsters, and other icky things. He looked in the closet, behind the curtains, in the toy chest, and under the bed. Tonight, as usual, everything was okay. So he jumped into bed and covered himself with the sheet.

But Adam wasn't sleepy — not just yet. He reached under his night table, where he found a flashlight, and a book of ghost stories that he had borrowed from the school library. He had been wanting to read it for a long time, but it was always checked out. Now, at last, it was his.

Adam held the flashlight over the book and read.

The Ghost of the Gray Wolf

Gitty Van Delft had never been this far from her home on Washington Square. But now she was almost ten and how shameful it was that she had never met her grandfather.

Grandfather did not like to leave his home far away up the Hudson River. And Father was always too busy with important bank business to make the trip. But Gitty thought there might be other reasons that had kept him away. Reasons no one ever told her about.

Gitty wore a new frock and bonnet, and Father said she looked like a great lady. She wanted her grandfather to find her pretty. She so hoped he would like her.

Father was often nervous, but during the train ride today, he was even more nervous than usual. He crossed his right leg over his left leg, then crossed his left leg over his right leg, then crossed his right leg over his left leg again.

He asked Gitty about her ice skates and told her about the pond near Grandfather's house where he skated as a boy. Then he asked her about her skates and told her about the pond again. Aside from that, he didn't have many words to share with his daughter during the long ride.

Gitty stared out the window at the high cliffs along the river. The scenery was very beautiful, but she was so eager to meet her mysterious relative, she could not enjoy it.

When they finally arrived, Gitty was surprised by her father's words. "I will return in a fortnight," he said. "Mind your grandfather. Make me proud of you."

Though the train station was crowded, Gitty found her grandfather right away. He had the same bushy brows, long nose, and thin lips as her father, but his hair was whiter and his forehead more wrinkled.

Grandfather led Gitty to a carriage drawn by two brown horses — one with a black mane and one with a white mane. Grandfather took the reins and they began a silent trip toward his house.

"What a pretty place." Gitty finally gathered the courage to speak as they entered the town.

"What you see is pretty enough," Grandfather said. "But there's more to things than what you see, Granddaughter. You must always remember that."

That night, safe within the solid brick walls of Grandfather's house, Gitty listened to the sounds from outside. She heard chirping crickets, singing sparrows, hooting owls, and rustling leaves.

"Owowowooooo . . . owowowooooo . . ."

"Is that the wind?" Gitty asked her grandfather.

"Some say it is the wind," he answered. "And some say it is the ghost of the gray wolf."

"Will I see wolves here?" Gitty asked.

"Not these days," said her grandfather. "But there was a time when wolves, not men, ruled this land.

"One day, a mother wolf left her cubs to look for food. Wolves are very good mothers, you know. Well, a farmer came by and discovered the cubs.

"'You look harmless enough now,' he said. 'But someday you will be big enough to kill my hens.' And he carried the cubs to the pond and drowned them.

"When the mother wolf returned, her cubs were gone. She searched and searched. She didn't eat or sleep. The mother wolf died, but she kept searching. And by the light of the stars, you can hear her call.

" '*Owowowooooo . . . owowowooooo . . .* ' "

"That's sad," said Gitty. "What happened to the farmer?"

"Every moment of every night, the farmer heard the howl. '*Owowowooooo . . . owowowooooo . . .*' He couldn't sleep; finally he went mad. One morning he was found drowned in the same pond where he had killed the cubs."

That night as she lay in bed, Gitty heard the sound.

"*Owowowooooo . . . owowowooooo. . . .*"

Is it the wind or is it the ghost wolf? she wondered as she drifted off to sleep.

The next morning Gitty dressed in the frosty chill of her room. She pushed open the shutter, and to her delight, saw the pond that her father had told her about. It was covered with a sleek white layer of ice. But the pond had to wait until late that afternoon, since Grandfather had planned a day of visiting.

"Be back before sundown," her grandfather warned as Gitty skipped out the door with her skates swinging behind her back.

12

Gitty found the best ice at the far side of the pond. She skated and skated. She skated forward. She skated backward. She fell down a few times when she tried a spin, so she tried again and again and again. Gitty was not aware of the time. The sun was going down, and she could begin to see the shape of the moon.

Gitty quickly took off her skates and walked across the pond. Her feet slipped and slid, but she somehow stayed up. Then she heard the sound.

"*Owowowooooo . . . owowowooooo . . .*"

Gitty looked over her shoulder and saw what she feared. A pale gray wolf with fiery red eyes.

"*Owowowooooo . . . owowowooooo . . .*"

The wolf panted heavily, showing her sharp teeth.

Gitty walked faster and faster. Her footing became less sure. Then *CRACK!*

Gitty could remember very little about what happened next. She felt cold water. . . something pulling her by her jacket. . . and howling.

"*Owowowooooo . . . owowowooooo . . .*"

Then she was in her room with her grandfather by her side.

"Who pulled me out?" Gitty asked.

Her grandfather shook his head. "We'll never know," he said.

But after that day, the ghost wolf was never heard again. She had found what she was looking for at the bottom of the pond.

Adam looked up from his book. A pattern of dark and light moved across the wall. Adam knew it was only a shadow that was made by the lights of a passing car. But just to be sure, he reached over to where he kept his ghostblaster and aimed for the wall.

Zap!

With that taken care of, Adam rolled over and went to sleep.

Chapter Three

ADAM GOT into the back of the blue station wagon. After he buckled up, Adam had to pull in the strap of the seat belt. Someone had let it out *very* far. Adam pretended to sound like Papa Bear. "Who's been sitting in *my* seat?" Adam asked.

"It was Aunt Ellen," said his mother.

Adam giggled. "Oh."

It was a clear crisp day, and Adam had lots of energy.

"I can feel that kicking against my back," said Mrs. Johnson.

"Sorry, Mom." Adam stopped his feet,

though they wanted to keep moving. "How come you're driving so slowly today?" Adam asked.

"I'm driving at the same speed I always go," said his mother.

They stopped at a stop sign for what seemed like a million years. Then they turned the corner. Oh, no, a red light!

"I think this traffic light might be broken," Adam said.

"It's not broken," said his mother. "Be patient."

Adam had very good eyesight. He could see what he was looking for from two blocks away. The tiny speck on the lawn in front of the yellow house was Chuck Webber.

"I've been waiting forever," said Chuck. "I already know every joke in this book. Why did the chicken cross the road?"

"To get to the other side," said Mrs. Johnson. "That's an old one."

"Okay, I've got another," said Chuck. "Why did the chicken cross the playground?"

"Oh, no," said Adam. Adam looked at the

cover of Chuck's book. *Fifty-five Farm Jokes* was the title.

"Why did the chicken cross the playground?" Chuck repeated. "Give up?"

"You've got me on that one," said Mrs. Johnson.

"To get to the other side of the playground," said Adam.

"Nope," said Chuck. "To get to the other slide. Get it? The other *slide*."

"I like my answer better," Adam said.

"But it's not the answer in the book," said Chuck. "So it's wrong."

The car slowed down when they reached the driveway of Blackwell House. The school's main building was very crowded, so the third grade went to school in this spooky-looking old house.

"Now, I want you to be good boys," said Mrs. Johnson as she drove down the curvy road. "Mind the teachers and the other grown-ups in charge."

"Aw, Mom," said Adam. "Is that any way to talk to a hero?"

Mrs. Johnson laughed. "Excuse me, Mr. Hero, but the hero's mother would like to remind her hero son and his hero friend to behave."

Adam and Chuck and four other third-graders became heroes earlier that year when they solved a mystery about their school-house. Strange things had happened at Black-well House. Pencils rolled off desks, lights flickered, things fell off shelves, doors rattled and slammed — all by themselves. Everyone thought that Blackwell House was haunted and that the ghosts didn't like sharing their house with the third grade.

Mr. Jenkins, their teacher, set up a committee to study the problem. Adam and Chuck were on it and so were Danny Biddicker, Joey Baker, Debbie Clark, and Norma Hamburger.

One night the boys and girls stayed overnight in the haunted schoolhouse. It was a scary night — but they found their ghost! And Adam and Chuck and the others got their picture in the newspaper.

As the blue station wagon pulled away, a brownish car pulled up in its place. A skinny girl with glasses sat next to the driver.

"Hey, Norma Hamburger," Chuck called. "Have you been to any barbecues lately?"

Chuck liked all kinds of jokes. He liked monster jokes, elephant jokes, knock-knock jokes, and now farm jokes. But his favorite jokes of all were hamburger jokes. He liked to tell them to Norma Hamburger.

Norma was the smartest girl in the third grade. She was quiet and shy, and she turned bright red when anyone said her last name. Chuck Webber teased her about it all the time. Norma hated that.

"Have a great time," Mrs. Hamburger called from the car. She did not tell Norma to be good. She did not have to. Norma was always good.

Chapter Four

MR. JENKINS STOOD by the door of the bus with a clipboard in one hand and a pen in the other.

"You can get on now," he said as he put a check next to Norma's name.

From Norma's eye level, it was hard to see who was sitting where. The high backs of the bus seats hid the children's faces. Norma was looking for Kim or Liz.

As she walked up the aisle, Norma's heart sank. She found them both. But they were sitting next to each other — whispering and giggling. Norma was left out of their fun —

again. She took a seat two rows behind them and waited for someone to sit next to her.

When Jeff Arnold got on the bus, Norma and the other kids with empty seats next to them slouched down. They wished they could make themselves disappear. Sitting next to Jeff for the whole bus ride would be horrible. Luckily Jeff didn't sit next to any of them. Instead he found two empty seats and spread himself out over both of them.

Jeff was the third-grade bully. He liked to pick on the littler kids. And next to Jeff, all the third-graders were littler — except for Danny Biddicker. Danny was the best athlete in the whole third grade. He was probably better than any fourth-grader, too.

Heads turned as Danny Biddicker got on the bus. He was surrounded by the sweet smell of freshly baked brownies. Danny carried two giant shopping bags. He wanted to be sure he had enough food for the whole trip — and that he had enough for every kid on the bus.

Mr. Jenkins got on the bus and counted heads. Then he looked at his list.

"We're just waiting for Debbie and Joey," Mr. Jenkins announced. "Then we'll be off."

"Joey is late because his family is at their vacation house on the moon," said Jeff. Everyone giggled. They all knew that Joey made up stories.

Then a tiny voice came from the very last seat on the bus. "I'm here." The voice belonged to Joey.

"How did you get on without me seeing you?" Mr. Jenkins asked.

"I was the first one here," said Joey. "I just got on."

A car horn honked. Debbie Clark ran onto the bus and plopped down next to Norma.

"Thanks for saving me a seat," said Debbie. She was still out of breath. "This is going to be a great trip."

"Yeah," said Norma. "We'll get to see all sorts of farm animals — chickens, pigs, cows, horses."

"Boring," said Debbie. "I'm going bug-watching." She pulled a book out of her knapsack. "This is a bug-watcher's diary. Pictures of all kinds of bugs are in this book. Every time I see a new one, I write down the date, the time, and the place. I've already found fourteen of the bugs in this book. If I'm lucky, I'll find five or six more on this trip."

From behind them came a small voice. "Once I was bitten by a tarantula, and I had to go to the hospital to get the poison out," Joey said.

"There are no tarantulas in this part of the world," Debbie said.

"Yes, there are," said Joey. "There is one at the zoo."

Norma and Debbie just shook their heads.

Mr. Jenkins sat down in the seat next to Mrs. Pick, and off they went.

Chapter Five

SOMEONE STARTED to sing "Old Macdonald Had a Farm" and everyone joined in. After a few rounds of "Row, Row, Row Your Boat," then "BINGO," the voices faded and stopped. Mr. Jenkins announced they were halfway there.

What bad luck! The beautiful spring day grew dark, and it started to pour. With all the clouds and rain, the children couldn't see out the windows. The bus driver turned on the lights in the bus, but they were very dim. The children grew quiet.

Jeff suddenly broke the silence. "Look."

He read a sign along the highway. " 'Exit to State Prison.' Have you heard the story about the escaped prisoner?"

"We certainly don't need to hear it now," said Mr. Jenkins.

"What escaped prisoner?" Joey whispered. Jeff ignored him.

"That's just an old story that counselors tell around a campfire to scare the campers," Debbie said.

Some of the kids thought they saw a strange light along the top of the bus.

"This is spooky," said Adam.

"Our trip is haunted," said Jenny Carle.

"Here we go again," said Debbie.

All of a sudden the bus swerved and came to a stop. The driver gasped and ran out of the bus. Mr. Jenkins followed him. Five minutes later, Mrs. Pick went to look for the bus driver and Mr. Jenkins. The children were left all alone.

Jeff Arnold reminded them of the State Prison nearby. "I'll bet a prisoner escaped and got the bus driver," he said. "And then he got Mr. Jenkins and Mrs. Pick. And now he's looking at the bus and waiting. Waiting to see who will come out next."

Kim and Liz giggled nervously. Lori Marino trembled. Joey started to cry.

"You're just making that up," said Danny. "Does anyone want a brownie?"

But no one felt like eating now.

Adam looked out the window, but it was too dark and rainy. He couldn't see a thing. In the distance, he heard a shrieking sound — like a scream . . . or a howl . . . or a siren. . . . Then Adam saw a flashing light. It was the police.

Chapter Six

JUST THEN Mrs. Pick returned to the bus.

"Everything is okay, kids," she said. "The bus driver had to drive off the road to avoid a deer. We got stuck in some mud. Luckily, the State Police were right behind us. We will be moving very soon."

The storm stopped as quickly as it started. Once again the bus was rolling under sunny skies. As the children got closer to the farm, they grew restless. Mr. Jenkins started the alphabet game.

"A — automobile," he said.

Each kid had to find something that began

with a letter. They went across the aisles, then up the rows. Meanwhile, Danny passed out brownies.

"B — bus."

"Cow."

"Dog."

It was Lori Marino's turn. "E . . . e . . . e . . ." she repeated. "Earth!"

"F — farm."

"Grass."

"House."

"I . . . i . . . i . . ." It took a long time for Adam to find something that began with the letter I. Finally, he found it. "Inn!"

Everyone cheered.

J was another hard one. Chuck almost got stuck on it, but he got lucky. "Junk!" he shouted. "Look at all the junk out there!"

Everyone cheered again.

It was Danny's turn and he had the letter K. He looked and looked, but he couldn't see one K word. He started to sweat. His face became red. This made him feel dumb, and he hated feeling dumb. He liked playing football. When he played football, he didn't feel smart or dumb. He just felt good.

Then he had an idea. "Knee!"

"That's not fair," said Kim. "You have to pick something outside the bus."

"It is so fair," said Norma. "Knee is a K word and Danny sees a knee."

Everyone in the bus had something to say about it. Finally Mr. Jenkins ruled on it.

"Knee is good," he said.

Some of the kids cheered and some of the kids booed. But Danny felt good.

"L — land," said Debbie.

Norma couldn't believe her bad luck. Something inside her forced her to give the answer. All eyes were on her — or on the building that was coming up on the right.

She said it at last. "McDonald's."

"Where Norma Hamburger gets together with her family," said Chuck.

And everyone laughed.

Chapter Seven

THERE WERE STILL five letters left in the game when it came to an end. The bus stopped in front of a big white farmhouse.

Two classes of fidgety eight- and nine-year-olds finally got a chance to stretch and jump and run.

The girls went to the bunks on one side of the farmhouse. The boys went to the bunks on the other side.

Adam, Joey, Danny, and Chuck were told to go to the first bunk. Only one bed was left. The boys had time to unpack and make their beds before they found out who would join them. Adam winced when he heard the nasty voice of Jeff Arnold.

"Move over, dorks," he said. "I'm bunking in here." He pointed to the bed that Joey had so carefully made up. "And that bed is mine."

Joey looked as if he were ready to cry. Danny helped him make up another bed, and they finished quickly.

It was time to see some of the farm. The third-graders went in groups of six. Adam's group went to the barn. Adam could have found the place blindfolded, the smell was so strong.

Two rows of cows were munching their cud as they were being milked. Adam had never been this close to a cow before. He stared and the cow stared back. Adam thought she looked bored.

Adam was getting bored, too. He wanted to have an adventure. He looked over to the other kids in the group. Norma Hamburger was listening very carefully while the farmer explained how the milking machines worked. Debbie Clark was looking for things on the ground. All of a sudden Joey screamed. Jeff had put a caterpillar on his arm. Adam didn't understand why Jeff would think that was funny. He wondered about kids like Jeff.

Chapter Eight

ADAM, CHUCK, AND DANNY had their dinner together. Chuck had already eaten three hot dogs and told four farm jokes.

"Why should you never tell secrets in a corn field?" he asked. This time, Chuck didn't even wait for an answer. "Because the corn has ears!"

Adam's mother didn't cook hot dogs. She said there was something bad in them. But Adam was allowed to eat them out.

When he did eat one, he really enjoyed it. He sniffed the sweet and spicy smell, then bit into the warm, juicy meat and the crispy bun.

Adam tried to eat slowly to make the feeling last longer. But that ruined the taste. When he was finished, Adam ate a second hot dog. But it wasn't as good as the first.

There were chocolate chip cookies for dessert. Adam was too full to eat his, so he wrapped it and took it to his bunk.

Inside, he had a strange sense that he wasn't alone. He thought he saw a light flash on the wall. Did he see it or didn't he? Adam wasn't sure.

But he didn't give it another thought. He quickly put the cookie away and ran out to join the others.

After dinner, Mr. Jenkins started a really crazy game of softball. Anyone could play — the students, the teachers, and the farmhands.

There were sixteen people in the outfield. About thirty others waited for a turn at bat. No one had any idea what the score was. But everyone was laughing and having a good time.

Sammy Baum was on third and Chuck was

on first when a small girl was being coaxed toward the batter's box.

"Hey, look," Chuck shouted. "It's Hamburger on the plate! Get it? Hamburger on the plate?"

Norma blushed and quickly struck out. Mr. Jenkins wanted her to have another try, but Norma didn't want to.

Adam was up next. He tried to keep his eye on the ball, but in the distance he saw an animal running. What was it? A dog? A wolf? Adam hit a pop-up to the shortstop. It should have been an easy out. But too many people went for it. They knocked into each other, and the ball got away. Adam ran to first and Chuck to second.

Then Dan smashed the ball and everyone ran home.

Joey usually didn't like softball. He hated going up to bat. Everyone would stare and watch as he struck out. But in this game he didn't have to bat. He just stayed in right field no matter which team was up. He could feel like part of the game without doing anything. Other kids were there to go after any ball that might come his way.

Jeff Arnold was up next. He hit a fly ball that landed right in Joey's glove. Joey couldn't have missed it if he tried.

"Out!" said Mr. Jenkins.

"Nice going," said Dan.

Jeff was mad. "I'll get you for this," he said.

What bad luck, Joey thought.

Joey had never caught a fly ball before. He wished he had missed this one, too.

Chapter Nine

THE BOYS WERE very tired. As they crawled into their beds, Joey whined. His legs were caught in the sheets. Jeff giggled.

The other boys guessed what happened. Jeff had short-sheeted Joey's bed. Adam, Chuck, and Danny pretended that nothing was wrong. They hoped Jeff would stop being a bully if they ignored him. And Danny helped Joey make up his bed . . . again.

Then the boys heard the sound.

"Owowowooooo . . . owowowooooo . . ."

"What's that?" Joey asked.

"It sounds like a wolf," said Danny.

"No way," said Chuck. "There aren't any wolves in this part of the country."

"There aren't now," said Adam. "But I'll bet there were lots of them a hundred years ago."

Then they heard it again.

"Owowowooooo . . . owowowooooo . . ."

Joey whimpered. Chuck covered his head with his pillow. Adam took out his notebook and wrote. *Friday. 8:53 p.m. Heard wolf howls. No wolves living in this part of the country.*

It was hard for Adam to fall asleep. He wanted to check the bunk the way he checked his room every night. He wanted to look under the beds and in the lockers. But he could not. He would not know how to explain it to the other boys.

That night Adam had a nightmare.

He was climbing a hill when it started to rain. He knew it was not safe to stay under a tree. So he looked for a place to go. At last he found a cave.

Adam crawled in. He was surprised to find a litter of newborn wolf cubs. They were so tiny he could pick one up in each hand. Adam stroked his cheeks with their soft fur. The tiny cubs seemed to enjoy his warm skin.

Then Adam heard the howl.

"Owowowooooo . . . owowowooooo . . ."

He looked up to see angry eyes and large teeth.

Adam gently put the cubs down, then ran as fast as he could. The wolf was close behind him. In his ear, Adam heard, *"Owowowooooo . . . owowowooooo . . ."*

She thinks I want to harm her cubs, Adam realized.

Adam's legs grew weak, and he felt as if he were moving in slow motion.

There were big rocks in his path. Tripping and stumbling, Adam ran through them. Then he fell.

When he opened his eyes the wolf was gone, the trees were gone, and Adam was back in the bunk.

But Adam still heard the howl.

"Owowowooooo . . . owowowooooo . . ."

Adam looked over to the other beds. Chuck and Joey were also awake. Jeff's bed was empty.

All of a sudden a dim light shone on the far wall. The light began to form a shape — the shape of an animal. Adam could not clearly see what kind. It could have been a wolf.

Then the form disappeared, and from outside, the boys could hear, *"Owowo-wooooo . . . owowowooooo . . ."*

"Did you see that?" Chuck asked.

"I saw it," said Adam.

Joey was too scared to say anything. But he had seen it, too.

Chapter Ten

THE WIND SHIFTED, filling the bunk with cow smells, cow bells, and mooing. The rooster crowed as darkness lifted from the bunk. A bright new day was about to begin.

Danny stirred.

"I can't believe you slept through all that," said Chuck.

"All what?" Danny asked.

Chuck filled him in as Adam wrote in his notebook. *Saturday. 5:18* A.M. *Heard howls. Saw animal shape on bunk wall. Also seen by Chuck Webber and Joey Baker. Danny Biddicker sleeping in bunk. Jeff Arnold missing from bed.*

"Do you think it was a real ghost?" Joey asked.

Adam hoped so. "It could be. Or it could be a fake ghost."

"Maybe someone is trying to play a trick on us," Danny said.

"Maybe that someone is Jeff Arnold," said Chuck.

"Right," said Adam. "So first we must find out where Jeff Arnold has been."

"Leave it to me," said Chuck. "I'm real good at getting people to talk."

The delicious smell of pancakes mixed with the sweet scent of hay as Chuck walked toward the mess tent. Chuck loaded his tray with pancakes, scrambled eggs, and toast, and took two cartons of chocolate milk. Then he looked around until he found what he was looking for — an empty seat next to Jeff Arnold.

Jeff was surprised. Chuck had never tried to be friendly before.

"Do you mind if I sit here, Jeff?" Chuck asked politely.

"Not at all, Charles," said Jeff. "Do you mind if I call you Charles?"

Chuck really hated it. "Of course not," he said. "So, where were you this morning?"

"What's it to you?" said Jeff.

"Just wondering," said Chuck.

"Well, it's none of your business," said Jeff. He picked up his tray and left Chuck to eat all by himself. "See you around, Charles."

Just then, Chuck felt something licking his elbow. A baby goat had somehow gotten into the mess tent. Chuck patted the baby goat on the head and gave it a piece of his toast.

"I'd rather have breakfast with you than with dumb old Jeff Arnold," Chuck said to the goat.

The brown colt was eating oats from Adam's hand. Adam imagined he was a cowhand in the wild west and this was his powerful, sure-footed pony. Adam thought about how nice it would be to have a horse. He'd trade one for his younger brother any day.

"Hey, Adam!" An excited voice broke into his daydream. The voice belonged to Chuck.

"I spoke to Jeff," said Chuck. "He wouldn't tell me where he was this morning. That proves it. He knows something about our ghost."

"That doesn't prove anything," said Adam.

Just then Danny showed up.

"Neat horses," Danny said, and he grabbed a handful of oats and fed them to a chestnut mare. "I found out why Jeff wasn't in his bed. He got homesick. He was with Mr. Jenkins."

"You're kidding," said Chuck.

"No, it's true," Danny said. "I told Mr. Jenkins we got worried when Jeff wasn't in his bed this morning. Mr. Jenkins told me himself."

"So Jeff Arnold had nothing to do with our ghost," said Adam. "This changes everything."

Chapter Eleven

ADAM CALLED A MEETING of the original ghost-hunting committee. Norma still held the note in her hand.

> *Meet after dinner.*
> *Ghost business.*
> *Very important.*

Debbie got the same note. "What's this about?" Debbie Clark was going to be a scientist when she grew up. And scientists don't believe in ghosts.

The boys told the girls what had happened in their bunk.

The girls looked at each other.

"How can we help?" Norma asked.

"I have a plan," said Adam. "Tonight, one hour after lights out, we meet outside our bunk.

"After we leave, one of us will measure where everything is in the room. That way we will know if a ghost has come and moved things."

"I'll do that," said Debbie.

Adam continued. "One of us will spread some flour on the floor and tables to find prints of any fake ghosts."

"I can do that," said Norma.

"Great," said Adam. "You carry the camera, Joey. If you see anything unusual, get a picture."

"Okay, Adam," said Joey.

"Chuck, you know how the tape recorder works. Use it if you hear anything strange."

"Gotcha," said Chuck.

"Danny, you can be the lookout. Warn us

if you see anyone — or anything — coming."

"And I'll take notes."

"What about Jeff?" Joey asked.

"I already told Jeff what we are doing. He promises to stay out of our way — if we promise not to tell anyone he was homesick."

"It sounds like a good plan to me," said Norma.

"It sounds good to me, too," said Danny.

Adam was very excited. Here was the adventure he was waiting for. "We did it before. We can do it again!" he said.

Chapter Twelve

ADAM LIVED in the suburbs, where the night was filled with lights: street lights, car lights, lights from windows and porches. In the country the night lights came from the moon and the stars. Tonight a full moon came out, but it was partly hidden by clouds. It was very dark.

Adam was frightened. But at least he wasn't alone. Chuck, Danny, Joey, Norma, and Debbie were with him.

Norma and Debbie worked inside the bunk as planned. When they were done they joined the boys outside.

The third-graders kept a close watch on the bunk. Nothing went out and nothing went in.

The children were very quiet. Around them they could hear the sounds of night animals. They rustled, they squeaked, they hooted, they chirped, they buzzed.

Norma wondered what might be crawling near her hand. Adam thought about what might be flying so close to his head.

Joey broke the silence.

"I'm getting sleepy," he said.

"Me, too," said Danny.

Soon all of them were having a hard time keeping awake.

"Let's tell stories," said Norma.

"I know one," Adam said softly. "In a dark, dark forest was a dark, dark house. And in the dark, dark house was a dark, dark room. And in the dark, dark room was a dark, dark closet. And in the dark, dark closet was a dark, dark shelf. And on that dark, dark shelf was a dark, dark box. And in that dark, dark box there was . . ."

"What was there?" Joey asked.

"Shh. I hear something," said Adam.

Everyone listened.

Twigs broke, leaves cracked. Footsteps were coming closer and closer and closer.

Norma hid her eyes in her knees. Debbie climbed a tree. Joey crawled under a bush. Danny joined him there. Chuck got down on his belly.

Adam just froze.

The footsteps were very near.

Chapter Thirteen

ADAM SAW A white form. It moved. Then Adam heard a giggle. He had heard that giggle before.

"I know it's you, Jeff Arnold," Adam said.

The giggle became a laugh. And Jeff pulled the sheet off his head.

"I sure had you scared. Didn't I, wimps?" said Jeff.

"That wasn't funny," Norma said.

Jeff kept laughing.

"No, that wasn't funny, homesick Jeff Arnold." Chuck was angry.

Jeff sneered. "You can say what you want.

No one will believe you. Not after I tell them
how scared you wimps were."

Still laughing, Jeff headed for the bunk.
When he got inside the laughing stopped.

"What's going on here?" he called.

The others came quickly.

"Wow," said Danny.

The rest were speechless.

Everything in the room was topsy-turvy.

Chairs were turned on their sides. Beds were undone. Mattresses were on the floor. All of Chuck Webber's clothes were thrown around the room.

"I'll get the kid who did this," said Jeff.

"No kid did this," said Norma. "Look!"

The flour she had spread on the floor was perfectly smooth. Not one footprint.

"A human would have left footprints," said Debbie. "This was done by a ghost!"

Chapter Fourteen

JOEY SNAPPED a picture. Chuck turned on the tape recorder. Adam wrote in his notebook. *Sunday. 12:34* A.M. *Mess in bunk. Clothes, beds, chairs, thrown around. No footprints or fingerprints. First seen by Jeff Arnold. Also seen by Chuck, Joey, Danny, Debbie, and Norma.*

Everyone helped fix up the bunk. Adam and Dan lifted mattresses. Joey and Debbie made up the beds. Jeff picked up the chairs. Norma swept the floor. Chuck folded his clothes. Soon everything was in place. But by now the children were too tired to wait for ghosts.

Norma and Debbie left the bunk, and the boys got ready for bed. But Adam could not fall asleep. He was disappointed. This was their last night on the farm. Now he would never know the truth.

Adam didn't even change into his pajamas. He just lay on his bed and stared into the darkness.

It was early in the morning — before the sun was up. From outside the bunk came the sound.

"*Owowowooooo . . . owowowooooo . . .*"

Chuck was the first to wake.

"*Owowowooooo . . . owowowooooo . . .*"

That was the sound they heard the first time the ghost appeared. Chuck wanted to wake the others, but he was too frightened to move.

"*Owowowooooo . . . owowowooooo . . .*"

Chuck kept his eyes squeezed tight. He was afraid of what he might see if he opened them.

"*Owowowooooo . . . owowowooooo . . .*"

Chuck wished the others would wake up, too. Maybe they were awake like him and were too scared to move, he thought. Or maybe they would never wake again.

"*Owowowooooo . . . owowowooooo . . .*"

Chuck heard the creak of the door. He couldn't take it anymore. He had to open his eyes.

And then he saw it . . . in the far corner of the room . . . the ghost wolf! Big shiny eyes . . . hanging tongue . . . sharp teeth. . . .

"*Owowowooooo . . . owowowooooo . . .*"

Chuck closed his eyes. When he opened them again, the ghost wolf was gone. He reached over to wake Adam. Adam was gone, too!

Chapter Fifteen

ADAM WAS ON HIS WAY to catch a ghost.

"I had a feeling it was you," he said. Adam stood with his arms crossed and stared.

"You are the only ones I know who are smart enough to do this. And you were the last ones in the bunk last night. You messed it up, then put the flour on the floor. I knew when Debbie said that a ghost did it. Debbie doesn't even believe in ghosts."

Norma blushed. She tried to hide the projector behind her back. But it was too late. Debbie, who held a tape recorder, giggled.

Danny, Chuck, Joey, and Jeff came outside. They were all very surprised.

"Let's see how you did it," said Adam.

Norma aimed the projector toward the bunk wall. A spot lit up. As she focused, the picture became clear. It was a picture of a wolf.

"I just made it go through that open window," Norma said.

Meanwhile, Debbie started the tape recorder. *"Owowowooooo . . . owowowooooo . . ."*

"Where did you get the idea for a wolf?" Dan asked.

"From a story I found in our school library," Norma answered.

"I know that story," Adam said.

"I got the slide and the tape at the museum when they had a special wolf show," Debbie said.

"That explains everything," said Chuck.

"No, it doesn't. Why did you do it?" Adam asked.

Norma grinned. "Chuck always makes fun

of my name. I got tired of his hamburger jokes."

"So we decided to play a joke on him," said Debbie.

"I didn't know it bothered you," said Chuck. "I won't do it anymore if it does."

Danny, Adam, and Joey also promised.

"But you're not off the hook for this," said Chuck.

"That's right," said Adam. "Someday, when you're in a dark, dark room in a dark, dark house in a dark, dark forest, you'll be all alone and all of a sudden . . . BOO!"

And everyone laughed.

When he got back to the bunk, Adam wrote in his notebook. *Sunday. 6:15 A.M. Solved the mystery of the ghost wolf. Caught Norma Hamburger and Debbie Clark in the act. I did it before. And I did it again!*

This book belongs to

Lindsay Horan